Zephyr of Wild Horse Island

Zephyr of Wild Horse Island

Jane Ayres

Zephyr Of Wild Horse Island
Copyright: © 2009 by Jane Ayres
Original title: as above
Cover and inside illustrations: © Asbjørn Tønnesen
Cover layout: Stabenfeldt AS

Typeset by Roberta L Melzl
Editor: Bobbie Chase
Printed in Germany, 2009

ISBN: 978-1-934983-35-5

Stabenfeldt, Inc.
225 Park Avenue South
New York, NY 10003
www.pony4kids.com

Available exclusively through PONY.

Chapter 1

The great gray stallion stared at the sea, watching as the waves hurled their fury at the unyielding rocks, and the sky darkened.

The island was his kingdom. It was a desolate landscape of prickly gorse and tough heather, the towering cliffs home only to countless sea birds. To the northeast a stream bubbled from a freshwater spring. The island was impassable except for one bay to the south, where the cliffs had crumbled and the rocks had formed a precious makeshift staircase onto the island. At the highest point was an ancient stone circle. A brooding quiet pervaded.

Facing the bay was the old house.

The stallion turned on his haunches and began to approach the house, but the sound of mares calling stopped him in his tracks. He hesitated. Although the mares were his priority something held him back, drawing him toward the dark, shadowy building. The events of the past few days flickered in his memory.

The mares called again and suddenly the gray stallion was gone, galloping back to his herd.

The old house was dilapidated, the timbers rotten, the roof leaking, the floor tiles cracked. An ornate brass knocker decorated the front door. It had not been used for a long time. There were few visitors to the island. The house was all that remained of Henry Absalom.

✳ ✳ ✳ ✳ ✳

Henry Absalom had once been a handsome man with strong, sharply chiseled features and dark searching eyes. But by the time he had reached his late seventies his once jet-black hair had turned white and hung in long unkempt tresses down his back, giving him the appearance of a wild eccentric. His craggy face had been weathered like the rocks, a landscape of lines and pits, every painful experience carved there.

When Henry had first seen the island some years

before he had harbored the idea of building a house himself. But on exploration of his primitive surroundings he found that this was unnecessary; a house was already there, neglected and empty. It struck him as some kind of bizarre Gothic folly. He knew nothing of the previous occupants, how they had come to be there or why they had left. He cared little if their ghosts remained. Henry supposed that somewhere he must have relatives, but they did not concern him. After his wife had died, all he cared about were his horses. They had been with him for as long as he could remember, well before the island.

Once, he had owned a stud farm with an international reputation, his horses prized for their beauty and stamina. Buyers from across the world had paid vast sums to own one of these creatures and Henry had been rich. But where all the money had gone, he neither knew nor cared. In his self-imposed exile, Henry Absalom rejected all human contact.

Up until last year, Henry had sold off a selection of his colts and fillies from time to time. This kept the horses down to a manageable number and also provided the needed income to keep the stable going. He conducted his business via the Internet, enabling him to do what was necessary while keeping his contact with people to a minimum. But from now on, he intended to keep all of his horses.

The stable block stood at a right angle to the house and was home to eight mares, two with foals. The last horse in the row of loose boxes was his favorite, his beloved stallion. Henry had raised him from a foal and named him Zephyr, since he was as fast as the wind. The horse was pure Arab, fifteen hands of silver gray, with streaks of black running through his silky tail and mane and distinctive black patches on his hocks and knees. His large, velvet eyes were set in a broad forehead, and his generous nostrils flared in the small muzzle. His neat gray ears pricked up when he listened to the old man's words. The stallion had never had man or saddle on his back and, like Henry, his fiery nature had scared away many a groom trying to tend him. But in Henry's hands the stallion became as gentle as a kitten. They were like father and son, and no man came between them.

Despite his age and ill health Henry had never failed his duties, feeding, watering and grooming his animals. He was their provider and doctor, his vast knowledge acquired from many years of experience. Hard food and fresh hay were shipped in from the mainland and left in the barn. The suppliers never stopped at the house or checked to see if the old man was well; his past aggressive behavior toward them had effectively warned them off. Henry's attorney arranged for them to be paid. In the past, Henry had hired people to help with the horses; if they did not stay, they were quickly replaced. Their job was to look after the mares – they were forbidden to touch Zephyr. But eventually they all made the same mistake. No one could resist trying to handle the magnificent stallion, but he would only respond to the old man, a fact they learned at a price. Many left with physical scars, as well as the brunt of Henry's wrath.

Now, the old man struggled with feed buckets until every horse was fed. Once finished, he leaned on Zephyr's door, panting, his breath rasping and harsh. The stallion twitched his ears in alarm, momentarily distracted from his all-important meal. Then his nose plunged back into the bucket of grain.

Henry regarded the great horse with deep affection. It had been an unusually still and peaceful night when Zephyr was born to the beautiful black mare Amra. The full moon had played on the silver waves while a tiny gray foal lay wrapped in its silken birth bag in the straw. The foal had gulped for air, and then its sides began to rise and fall regularly as it started to breathe properly.

Amra had turned to stare at it before scrambling to her feet. The cord joining them broke apart. The foal had thrashed its spidery legs and struggled to stand up. After two wobbly attempts it succeeded. Amra tried to mop her son dry with her tongue, and when the cleaning was over she guided him to her milk. Henry had felt a surge of joy and relief. It had been a difficult pregnancy and the foal had been late arriving, but the wait had been worthwhile.

Walking back to the house to rest, Henry felt nostalgic as he relived the five years of Zephyr's life, of their battles as Henry sought to win the colt's trust, of their arrival at mutual respect, and finally, of the deep and loving bond that formed between man and horse. These days, he felt overwhelmingly tired much of the time, and the headaches that had plagued him recently had become far worse, almost unbearable at times. That concerned him. He decided to turn out the horses later that afternoon. It was a simple arrangement; Henry turned them loose on the island, and in the evening, he called and Zephyr, leader of the herd, would bring them all back. Although there were no clocks on the island, they kept strict time. Once a routine was established the horses kept to it.

In the distant past, Henry had ridden some of his

horses to exercise them, but a back injury had put an end to that so he had to rely on the horses exercising themselves. He persuaded his aching legs to take him up the stairs and sank onto the creaking bed. His thoughts were troubled. Doubts about his ability to care properly for the herd in his condition increased daily. But right now, he needed to sleep.

Outside, clouds had gathered and as the afternoon wore on, the skies became dark and threatening. The horses moved about nervously in the stable. Zephyr thrust his head over the half-door of his box, sniffing the air. He was agitated. Henry should have let them out hours ago. The stallion pawed the ground impatiently, shaking his head. He uttered a loud urgent whicker.

The old man slept on. He was dreaming as he had never dreamt before. Turbulent, disturbing pictures in vivid color. His breathing quickened as he tossed from side to side, moaning and muttering. He saw his life being twisted and distorted, the images confusing until, finally, he awoke with a blood-curdling, desperate scream. He sat bolt upright, listening to the sound of his own labored breathing.

Minutes passed before he noticed a woman calling to him, clear and bell-like. Henry smiled as he recognized his wife's voice. It was unmistakable. At last she had come for him.

Still dressed, he rose from the bed and followed the voice across the landing and down the creaking wooden staircase. He reached the bottom almost breathless with effort. Although he waited, the house was again silent. Sighing, he leaned against the banister, tears stinging his cheeks. She had not waited. He was alone again. He opened the door to the kitchen, feeling suddenly very thirsty, when the sharp pain to his head came, worse than ever before. His vision blurred, his eyes hurt. Through his shock and agony, Henry knew that before he left he must take care of his horses. He stumbled outside, the pain increasing.

Zephyr heard his footsteps, uneven and faltering, and whickered a greeting. One by one Henry slid the bolts back until every door of the stable block was open. The mares stood huddled in the yard. Up above, the storm had broken and a rumble of thunder persuaded them to head for the shelter of the trees. The rain poured down from the black night sky, but Zephyr remained in the doorway of his box, watching as the old man leaned for support on the door. Henry gestured weakly with his arm, and the stallion trotted a few steps into the yard before stopping again.

"Go," murmured Henry. "There's nothing for you here now. You have to fend for yourself." Every breath hurt and the rain soaked through his body, chilling his bones. Still the horse lingered, sensing Henry's pain, reluctant to leave him.

Then Henry heard the woman's voice calling him again, so near she could have been standing beside him, and he knew that time was running out. He must make Zephyr understand. The pain was overwhelming him. He drew on his last reserves of strength.

"Go!" The scream echoed through the night as Henry used his last breath to tear the words from his throat.

Zephyr stared down at the crumpled body lying in the mud, the long white hair plastered to the face, the glazed eyes staring up at the empty sky. He took a tentative step forward. The smell of death stung his nostrils, and he backed away nervously. But then he stretched his neck down again and breathed in the old man for the last time.

Suddenly a fork of lighting lit up the sky and Zephyr turned and galloped away, anxious to find his mares.

Chapter 2

Zephyr picked his way through peat bogs and over rocky outcrops, calling his mares, furious that they had dared to leave without him. The chestnut, Chandra, replied, and he joined them under an overhanging rock and nipped Chandra to show his disapproval. When he was satisfied that they were all safe, he sheltered with them until the ferocious storm had subsided.

The horses spent the next day grazing under Zephyr's supervision. He felt unsettled and paced around, agitating the mares. When evening approached he waited expectantly for Henry to call, as he always did, so that Zephyr could bring the mares home.

Many nights passed before the stallion ceased to await the old man's call. He would not return to the house. The smell of death still lingered in his memory.

The herd knew where the best grass could be found, where the freshwater spring was located, and where to find shelter. But they were also used to the comfort of a warm stable when they needed it, banked with straw and hard feed to supplement their diet. They couldn't have known then that their first winter alone on the island would be exceptionally cold.

Zephyr's herd was highly bred and sensitive, and it would be a while before the offspring developed thicker coats and stronger teeth to adapt to the cold weather and rough winter diet. Still, each new generation would be tougher and more resilient.

As in all herds, responsibilities were divided so that while some horses grazed, others kept watch, ready to give warning at the slightest indication of danger. When the watchers finished their shifts they changed duties so they, too, could eat. Teamwork was essential for their survival.

They established a daily routine; they grazed in scattered groups with Zephyr to the side of the herd, close enough for them to unite at the first sign of trouble.

The herd had to eat enough to put on a healthy layer of fat that would last all winter, so that when spring arrived, they would be lean and trim.

✳ ✳ ✳ ✳ ✳

The feed supplier arrived later than usual from the mainland. A combination of inhospitable sailing weather and a heavy workload had pushed Henry's needs aside. As he dragged the first heavy load up to the barn, Bill Yates cursed at its weight and at the clammy damp that stuck to his clothes. He hated having to come to the island, which he regarded as hostile in every way. However, he was paid more than enough for his trouble; "danger money," the attorney had called it. Indeed, bad weather made the journey from the mainland treacherous. He had heard some unnerving stories about the old man but had only actually seen him once. Henry Absalom had seemed to him a strange figure, with his flowing white hair and stern eyes.

He leaned the sack against the barn door and straightened his back. He noticed that the stable doors were open and the horses out. They were usually there in the mornings, their inquisitive faces surveying the visitor. He felt disappointed, cheated even, that he had come all this way and not gotten a glimpse of the Arab stallion.

16

Then he saw the old man's body slumped by the door of Zephyr's box.

He shuddered. Had the stallion kicked Henry to death? Gingerly, he stepped forward. He bent over the body, afraid of what he might see. But he soon realized that Henry had been dead for some time and had not been attacked. Probably natural causes, he decided. Straightening up, it occurred to him that he was probably the only person to know that Henry had passed away. He looked at the sack of grain. He received regular payments into his bank account for supplying horse feed to the island and would probably continue to do so even if he never delivered another sack. He could keep the money without ever having to return. It would not be stealing, he told himself, since the old man was dead and the money no good to him. He nearly convinced himself that he was doing nothing wrong, but as he walked back to his boat, he changed his mind and decided to alert the police – after he had received his next monthly payment.

As time passed the horses forgot all their domestic habits and quickly adapted to their wild state. Zephyr was unquestioningly their leader, but the mares established a pecking order as well. Chandra, the chestnut, was the dominant mare, being the strongest. Her younger sister, the liver chestnut filly, Zoë, at first challenged her position but after a token display of aggression accepted her inferior status. But if Chandra were to display any sign of weakness in the future, Zoë would be ready to challenge her again. This was how status was established. No position was permanent. The stronger animals were responsible for the weak and vulnerable, and a member of the herd could only feel secure if it knew its exact place within the hierarchy. These were ancient instincts.

The only other male in the herd was Chandra's colt foal, and at eight months old, he would pose no threat to Zephyr yet. The colt would take his mother's rank at birth, and when he was a yearling he would test the other yearlings in play, in preparation for his future. It was essential that the stallion was strong and intelligent; a weak leader would endanger the herd. But Zephyr was a fine leader, powerful and alert.

By the time the first snow fell, the horses had already grown thick winter coats. Their very fine hair curled closely to their skins and was covered by longer coarse hair. The snow was unable to penetrate to their skins so eventually it dropped off as the horse's body heat melted it.

The herd had already resorted to eating twigs from young bushes, trees and even bitter and prickly plants that would have been previously ignored. They would dig into the earth to eat roots, or through layers of soft snow to munch at whatever lay beneath it. Chandra taught her colt to puff out the warm air from his nostrils to melt a hole in the snow to find food. He would feel delicately with his lips, his whiskers frost-covered, for a blade of grass or meager plant.

The water from the spring had frozen over, so each time they needed to drink Zephyr would first smash the sheet of ice with his hoof until water surfaced. He supervised the herd, and when they had finished he would drink too.

For weeks the wind and snow came down mercilessly, and at night, when the temperature was at its lowest, the horses would huddle together for warmth.

But eventually the snow began to thaw, leaving behind hard-baked ground with sparse brown grass for the horses to nibble at. The morning frosts became less severe until finally spring arrived. The herd had survived the trials of winter, though they were all much leaner for it, and the fresh spring grass was welcome.

The two foals were now yearlings. Chandra's colt was bright chestnut like his mother, and the filly shared

19

Zephyr's silver-gray coat. He had a son and daughter to be proud of, and three other mares were soon to foal.

It was a brisk and sunny morning when the first boat arrived. A rare golden eagle had been sighted on the island and poachers hoped to steal the valuable eggs to sell. Luckily the eagle had nested elsewhere, on a distant island. But the poachers, who knew nothing of Henry Absalom and his horses, caught a distant glimpse of Zephyr standing on a high and craggy rock, overlooking the herd.

They were both amazed and thrilled and watched for a while, unseen by the stallion at first. But the minute he caught their scent he signaled to the herd, and in seconds they had vanished into the trees. Although these men had no experience with horse trapping, they had contacts that stole for international buyers, who were prepared to pay a premium to get what they wanted.

Another week passed and the horses felt secure and safe on their remote island, protected by the unpredictable high winds that had dashed many a boat on the rocks. It was a warm day; a breeze fluttered through the trees, and the mares grazed contentedly. Zephyr stood slightly apart from the herd, resting his hind leg and apparently dozing.

Suddenly he lifted his head, flared his nostrils and breathed in deeply. He sensed that something was wrong and gave a loud whinny. The two yearlings fled to their mother's side and the mares crowded together for safety, watching Zephyr intently. Overhead, what sounded like a large swarm of very angry bees grew louder until it was deafening. The trees swayed and the grass flattened as the helicopter hovered above them. The horses snorted in terror and Zephyr signaled to them to flee, galloping at their head.

On this occasion, the men were merely inspecting the goods, ensuring that the stallion was worth the effort. Satisfied, they flew away, leaving the island in peace, at least until they had finalized their plans.

Chapter 3

Two days later, the herd was drinking at the stream with Zephyr standing guard, alert to the first sign of danger. His concentration was interrupted when Chandra and Zoë started to squabble. Just as he stepped in to intervene, nipping both females, there was a deafening sound overhead. He looked up at the skies, remembering.

The herd panicked, thrashing and splashing in the water. Quickly, Zephyr took control, and the horses galloped west in an instinctive attempt to outrun the flying creature. But the helicopter pilot was skilled and experienced and soon managed to split the herd into fragmented groups. The poachers knew their best chance of getting to the stallion was to separate him from the mares. To make their task easier, they intended to tire out their quarry.

Within a short space of time, the herd had dispersed and Zephyr was galloping alone. The helicopter hovered close overhead, the noise of the rotors thundering. Zephyr stretched his neck and lengthened his stride further, the scent of danger strong in his nostrils. He sensed there would be safety under the rocky crags, but the poachers anticipated his every move and each time he changed direction and headed for the rocks, they maneuvered to steer him away again. The chase went on and Zephyr stretched himself to his limits, sweat lathering his neck and sides in a thick white foam. Just as he started to flag, they steered him toward an outcrop of high boulders forming three sides of a jagged wall. Too late, Zephyr realized he was cornered. He reared up in fury and fear, challenging the fearsome giant flying insect. Turning to face his enemy he prepared to charge, baring his teeth. But before he knew it, a tranquilizer dart was released from a gun, stopping him in his tracks. He squealed in anger and surprise, but the drug took swift effect and very soon, everything went black.

It was many hours before Zephyr awoke, a long way

from the island and his mares. He blinked in the darkness of his strange new stable on the mainland, breathing in the unfamiliar smells and irritated by the nylon head collar that he now wore. He was unsteady on his feet, feeling weak and disorientated from the after-effects of the tranquilizing drug. He pawed the sawdust-covered concrete floor and sniffed around for water, but none was provided in his musty, cramped surroundings.

He was left alone overnight and finally, late the next morning, he heard the sound of feet on gravel outside and bolts sliding across the top half of the stable door. A man's voice, curt and rough, muttered, "Here's your breakfast," and a bale of hay was tossed over the door, which was quickly bolted again, shutting out the light. Zephyr sniffed the hay cautiously. It was dusty and poor quality, but he was hungry so he ate.

Throughout the day he heard footsteps and men's voices, but no one came near him until the evening. The door opened and two shadowy figures loomed in the doorway, their clothes reeking of tobacco. One shone a flashlight in his eyes while the other placed a bucket of water in the corner.

"I told you he was a looker," said one of the men. "I've already got a buyer, prepared to pay the right price."

26

"We'll need to get him out of here in the next few days. Remember, Wes, he's in your care, and I don't want him marked. I know your temper."

"Don't worry, I know how to handle him."

They laughed and turned, and the door slammed shut. As soon as their footsteps had receded, Zephyr drank the water, his thirst unbearable.

He paced around the small stable into the early hours of the morning, hating to be confined. Resentment built up inside him and by the time the man called Wes arrived, the stallion was in a terrible mood. The door opened and Wes tossed another bale of hay in. But the minute Zephyr bent his neck to eat, Wes grabbed the head collar, slipped a rope through it and tethered Zephyr to a ring in the wall, tying the rope as short as possible.

"I've got to muck out this stable and I don't feel like getting kicked," he growled, setting to work with a pitchfork. Zephyr eyed him with fury, ears laid back flat as he sought an opportunity to get his revenge. But Wes was clever and careful not to come within an inch of the stallion's sharp hooves.

Wes was just finishing the job when his cell phone emitted an irritating buzz.

27

"Darn it, of all the times to ring." For a split second Wes was distracted, laying the pitchfork down to reach for his phone. That was enough time for Zephyr. He strained on the rope and swung his quarters around as far as he could, pushing Wes off balance and straight into the wheelbarrow of horse dung. Swearing and cursing loudly, Wes grabbed the pitchfork and swung it at the horse. The wooden handle landed hard on Zephyr's shoulder and he screamed in pain. Wes was about to take another swing when he remembered his boss's order, that the horse must not be marked, and flung the pitchfork down on the wheelbarrow in disgust, glaring angrily. Swearing once more at the horse, he pushed the wheelbarrow outside and the door was hastily bolted again. Zephyr winced from the bruise that was forming on his shoulder. He was hungry but the hay was out of reach, tantalizing him. He was thirsty too, but the rope was so short he could hardly move his head at all. His neck soon ached, but Wes had no intention of releasing him for some time.

Many hours later, another man entered the stable, threw a blanket over Zephyr's head, nervously cut the rope that held him and left. Bewildered, the horse shook the blanket off and painfully stretched his stiff neck down to the water. He was determined never to let Wes near him again.

He listened attentively for Wes's return the next morning and when the bolts were slid back, he was ready.

Wes didn't get a chance to see what had hit him. The door had barely opened when the gray stallion charged at it and sent Wes rebounding backwards. He landed flat out in the yard. Delighted by his newfound freedom, Zephyr froze for a moment so that his eyes could become accustomed to the light. He stared around him. He was in a small yard by a row of four stalls. At one end of the yard was a dingy mobile home and at the other was a high wall, impossible to jump. The yard was encompassed by a barbed wire fence. Zephyr paced the length of the fence. He had not encountered barbed wire before and only considered the height of the fence. There was not enough room to jump the fence head-on – he needed to take a run at it, which would mean jumping it from an angle. He turned. He was still confused and perturbed at his unfamiliar surroundings, but he knew he had to get away from this place. He circled the yard once, then prepared himself. He took only four strides, and then launched himself into the air. His forelegs cleared it, but his hind legs trailed, catching the sharp barbs. He somersaulted, the sharp wire tearing at his hind legs, leaving long gaping wounds. He rolled over twice before struggling to his feet. Despite the searing pain, instinct compelled him to gallop onwards and leave the poachers as far behind as possible. His only thought was to return home to his mares, unaware that the island was over a hundred miles away.

Chapter 4

Stretching ahead were miles and miles of flat, desolate land. The poachers had ensured that their hideout was far from civilization. Zephyr kept on, lost and confused and heading for nowhere, knowing only that he must get away. When the rain poured down at noon he forged on, his pace slowing to a canter. There was no shelter in this wasteland and the water beat down mercilessly, running over his sides in rivulets. By dusk, he was walking, his hind legs stiff. The blood had dried and congealed over the deep wounds.

Eventually, he reached a road. It was little used, except to link two remote farms. He walked on the verge, pausing only to snatch a mouthful of grass. In the half-light he did not see the approaching car, and the driver, who was on his cell phone, did not see the horse until the last minute. He slammed on the brakes, the tires squealing, but the car just touched Zephyr's shoulder – not enough to injure, but sufficient to shock. The gray stallion was momentarily stunned but as soon as the car door opened, he took to his heels and disappeared into the distance before the driver had time to see him properly.

Zephyr spent a miserable night alone and shivering, resting his injured hind legs in turn. But when the sun began to rise he could hardly put any weight on the off-hind leg that had been more badly cut when had had jumped over the barbed wire, and he limped painfully. His progress was slow, but after traveling on further, he smelled a familiar and welcome scent and he stopped, ears pricked forward.

Mares.

Zephyr lifted his head, his nostrils drinking in the new scent. With renewed vigor he quickened his pace.

Up ahead, in a large railed paddock, grazed a dozen Thoroughbred brood mares, some with foals at foot. Zephyr forgot his pain and rushed forward to introduce himself. A couple of mares responded to his call and nickered, trotting over to the fence to investigate the stranger. The fence was too high for Zephyr to jump so he had to be content to remain on the outside of this unexpected harem.

Suddenly there was a scream of fury and Zephyr turned to see the stallion, who was being led out for morning exercise by the stud owner, Gwen Winters. She froze as the two horses surveyed each other, their bodies quivering. Although she was a strong, wiry woman, she knew she would be completely unable to hang on to her stallion, and within seconds he had pulled the rope through her hands. She watched as the animals sized each other up – Zephyr the proud gray intruder, and the herd's leader, a Thoroughbred at his peak, muscles rippling beneath the sleek black coat. His ears were laid flat, his eyes hostile. He reared high into the air, warning Zephyr to take flight. To his fury, Zephyr returned the challenge. The black opened his jaws and screamed again, his tone harsh.

The two now stood about eight yards apart, both half-rearing and squealing threats as they prepared for the fight. Although Zephyr was tired and wounded and therefore was the weaker of the two, he was prepared to win this new family, having lost his own. When the two horses charged and crashed together, their necks

entwining, Gwen ran back to the house and shouted for help. Her concern was for her valuable stallion and the damage that would almost certainly befall him. She had worked for many years to build up her precious stud and refused to lose her foundation, her mighty stallion. She cursed under her breath at irresponsible owners who did not keep their animals under control. She returned with her husband and the stable hand, waving pitchforks and shouting. But the stallions were locked in battle, their front legs striking and flailing, and Gwen noticed with anger that her stallion had a jagged cut on his neck.

"Do something!" she yelled at her husband.

"I'll get the gun," he said quietly.

Compelled to watch, Gwen could see that the gray intruder was losing the battle. Blood flowed from a fresh wound on his shoulder as the black lashed out with his hind legs.

"The gray's already injured," observed her husband, aiming the gun.

"Of course he is," snapped Gwen.

"No, I mean a previous injury. Look at his back legs. Dried blood."

Gwen followed his gaze. "You're right. Our stallion will kill him." The black's teeth stabbed and tore and

Zephyr knew that he was losing. The only way out would be to admit defeat. Dan Winters prepared to shoot, but Gwen turned to her husband. "It's all right. You won't need it after all."

They watched in grim, relieved silence as Zephyr turned on his heels and limped away, pursued by the triumphant black Thoroughbred.

Once Zephyr was safely off the Winters' land the black gave up the chase, satisfied that his point had been made and that the intruder would not return.

By now Zephyr was exhausted and thirsty, and his shoulder burned from the wound inflicted by the stallion. He wandered on, losing all track of time and distance, until eventually he could go on no longer. Giving up, he sank to the ground, his neck outstretched, longing for sleep. When morning came around again his body was stiff and he had no strength to stand. He gave a deep sigh and closed his eyes.

But unknown to Zephyr, he was being watched.

Chapter 5

Thom Sayers was thin, pale and seventeen years old with dark, spiked hair and watery gray eyes. He should have been at school, but he was sick of his bullying classmates so he had decided to go for a walk instead. He had no desire to participate in a double period of sports. He loathed sports and the humiliation of team picking. No kid wanted him on his team, and he was always the last boy to be chosen amid groans. He had never enjoyed competing with his peers and had no concept of team spirit, all of which did not make him popular with the other boys. He loved reading books that took him into worlds of imagination and fantasy and far exceeded his dull existence. A boy that preferred reading to sports, hip-hop music and computer games was not considered cool. Lately, with school exams looming, the topic of conversation had been extended to jobs and college, other subjects that offered no appeal or interest to Thom Sayers.

But as he cut across the common, Thom the loner realized that he was not alone that morning. Seeing Zephyr lying there from a distance he thought at first that someone's cow had escaped, so disguised was the creature by mud and dirt. Then, as he stepped nearer, he realized with astonishment that it was a horse. On closer inspection, he saw that the horse's eyes were closed and noticed the dried blood and matted hair. He felt sure the injured creature must be dead, but then Zephyr emitted an anguished sigh, and Thom knew he had to do something to help. He knelt down and stroked the horse's neck. It was cold to the touch.

"Poor thing," he murmured. "I have to get you up on your feet." He took off his jacket and laid it over the horse's neck. Zephyr opened his eyes and looked up in surprise at this pale young boy. He was too weak to fight.

Taking hold of the ragged head collar, Thom said firmly, "Come on, get up." Zephyr responded by lifting his head, then falling back again, but Thom did not give

in easily and tried again, coaxing and soothing. Finally, in a mighty heave, Zephyr struggled to his feet and stood shivering. His fear and hatred of mankind temporarily forgotten, the stallion allowed the boy to lead him back to his home on the outskirts of town, a sprawling, undistinguished place. The Sayers occupied a modern house on the edge of a new housing development. It was conveniently located near the shops, only a short car ride away, but it still offered a semblance of country life. They had moved to the area a year ago to get away from the congested city, with its high cost of living and constant traffic and pollution. The house backed onto an acre of unused land that his parents had bought with the intention of eventually splitting it into several plots. He doubted this plan would ever see fruition. His parents, both tutors at the local college, were out most evenings and weekends. The irony of the subject they taught still amused him – Sports Studies. And as if that wasn't enough, they spent their spare time at the local gym or the martial arts school, which left no time for other activities.

As Thom walked up the driveway he heard the sounds of the radio drifting through the open window and guessed that his grandmother was puttering around in the kitchen. She was his mother's mom, a fit and active woman in her early seventies who had been living with them for the past few years. She did most of the cooking and housework and took care of all of them. Thom sometimes wondered if his parents saw her as an unpaid housekeeper. She smiled at him through the window, and at his approach put aside the washing she was sorting to open the door.

"Hi, Gran," he said, smiling at the short plump woman standing before him in the doorway, her long gray hair wound into a thick braid around her head. He had always admired her long hair, which reached to her waist, and he remembered how his grandfather, her late husband, would brush it for her each morning.

"Shouldn't you be at school, Thom?" she asked, adding curiously, "Why is there a horse in the yard?"

"I found him," he explained. "He was lying in a field. I thought he was dead."

"He doesn't look very lively," she said. "He needs help."

"That's why I couldn't leave him."

"Okay. I'll get some hot water and towels. Those wounds need to be cleaned."

They spent the rest of the morning attending to Zephyr and doing their best to make him more comfortable.

"He's a very handsome horse," commented his grandmother. "Finn would have known what to do with him."

His late grandfather, Finn Miller, had loved animals and kept dogs, cats, goats, ferrets and horses on his farm many years ago. Thom had always loved spending his vacations on the farm when he was a child. They were his happiest memories.

They left Zephyr in the garden with layers of blankets fastened to his back and neck while his grandmother phoned the vet.

"He's busy right now, but he will come over as soon as he can," she said.

"Do you think the horse could have run away from somewhere?" wondered Thom.

"Maybe. Who knows? I haven't noticed any ads for lost horses in the local paper, but someone must own him. He looks valuable."

Thom knew she was right, but for the time being he wanted the horse to stay with them. There was something special about him; he sensed it.

When Thom's parents returned home, he had already converted the tool shed into a makeshift stable for the horse.

"Why are all my tools scattered all over the driveway?" asked his father, emptying his briefcase and putting the sweaty clothes straight into the washing machine.

"I'll put them in the garage. There's plenty of room," replied Thom casually.

"You haven't answered your father's question," said his mother as she hunted for her new sneakers.

"Because there's a horse in the shed," replied Thom, shrugging his shoulders as if this were an everyday occurrence.

"I don't think I heard you correctly." She raised her eyebrows.

"Thom rescued a horse today. It could have died. I think we should be proud of him," said Gran, anticipating an argument.

"Have you contacted the police?" asked his mother, the question mark almost visible over her head.

"Gran did. They didn't have any lost horses on their records. Maybe he hasn't got an owner," replied Thom. "Maybe he's wild."

"Don't be ridiculous. Anyway, you can't possibly be thinking of keeping him," said his mother.

"Why not?" Thom's voice was suddenly defensive. "We've got an acre of unused land…"

"But we haven't got a stable."

"I converted the shed. It took me all day."

"So you haven't been to school again?" His father frowned.

"This was more important," answered Thom.

"How many times do we have to tell you that a good education is the most important thing? You never listen! Poor school reports, mediocre academic ability… and you show no aptitude for sports!"

Thom, who had heard this countless times before, looked to his grandmother for support, but she was making coffee in hopes that it would calm things down before another argument ensued.

"If you ask me, you don't even try," continued his father.

A grim silence followed. Then Thom's mother said, as she often did, "Your father and I don't wish to discuss this further. We have a karate class to get to. Subject closed."

Thom wanted to scream and shout at them, but he knew that it would do no good. He scowled and glared and stormed out of the house, slamming doors loudly. Shaking with anger, he went to check on the horse. The creature still looked subdued and weak and Thom's rage subsided in an instant. He rubbed the horse's gray ears gently and felt sad inside. His parents had never allowed pets. His mother had not enjoyed being brought up surrounded by animals on a farm and had vowed that no non-human creature would share her own house. Thom buried his face in the horse's mane, breathing in the creature's warmth. He began to feel calmer, but he couldn't help wishing things were different.

When he went back into the house, his grandmother was sitting on the sofa, watching her favorite TV show.

"The vet has been called out to an emergency, but he will be here early tomorrow morning," she told him. "And I also called the animal charities to see if anyone had reported a horse missing. No one has."

"Thanks."

"Don't worry, Thom, things will sort themselves out. One step at a time. The priority now is to get the horse checked out and examined by a professional. Don't you agree?"

He nodded.

"Good. Now, come and sit here by me and watch TV."

Despite her words, by the next morning Thom felt as if a cloud of gloom hovered over him. He hated having to go to school, but worst of all was the thought that he could not keep the horse, even for a little while. What would happen if no one claimed him? Would he go to an animal shelter? Then what? Would he be destroyed? He couldn't bear the thought of that. It made sense for the horse to stay with him. But that wasn't going to happen.

His mother looked up from her cereal. "We've all had a talk about that horse. Despite our misgivings, your Gran seems to think it would be a good idea for you to keep the horse for the time being – if no one claims him, of course. She thinks it would be a useful hobby. Who knows, you might turn out to be a rider. You could be a sporting champion yet." She smiled awkwardly.

Thom wondered if she was feeling guilty for spending so much time away from home at endless sporting events. She would have these pangs every now and then and try to make up her absence by buying him gifts like chocolate or CDs. The horse wasn't any different, but he guessed that this change of heart was due to his grandmother. She could work miracles with his mom. Gran was amazing. What would he do without her?

"Thanks," he said quietly, although inside he was bursting with excitement.

"Your father will pay the vet's bill," added his Mom. "Now, I have to be going. Do you want a ride?"

Thom shook his head.

"Okay, but promise me you will go to school today?"

"Promise. See you tonight," he said.

"I've got a Parents' Evening, so I'll be late." She scooped up her car keys.

"Okay. Bye, Mom."

He sat at the kitchen table, grinning into his orange juice, unable to believe his luck. Now, he had to hope no one turned up to claim the horse.

"Everything all right?" asked his grandmother as she shuffled in, still wearing her dressing gown, her hair loose.

"Great, thanks to you."

"I'm glad. Would you braid my hair for me, Thom? Will you have time before you go to school?"

"I've always got time for you, Gran," he replied, hugging her.

Knowing that he had something to look forward to at home made the school day more bearable for Thom. He thought about the horse constantly. When he returned home later, the vet had come and gone. He'd given the horse an anti-tetanus injection and left ointment and cream to be rubbed onto Zephyr's wounds to heal the infection.

"We need to clean the cuts and put fresh dressings on daily. The cuts on his hind legs will heal in time.

The shoulder wound is deeper, so it will leave a scar. He needs rest, care and good food," said Gran. "We can manage that, can't we?"

Thom nodded. "If he's staying, I'd better give him a name. I thought about it at school today. I'm going to call him Finn. After Granddad."

Over the next few weeks Zephyr recovered his strength, and as the wounds healed and his coat became glossy, Thom could see what a magnificent creature he was.

The boy spent every waking minute with the horse, which gradually began to answer to the name of Finn. Thom dreaded a phone call telling him that the horse's owner had turned up and wanted his horse back, but as time passed he felt more confident that this would not happen.

As soon as he was strong enough, Finn was turned out in the field behind the house. He had gotten used to wearing a rope halter and although the memory of man's ill treatment remained, the horse knew that this boy was no threat to him and allowed himself to be handled.

"He's looking good these days," Gran commented one morning. "He gallops around like a wild thing, kicking

up his heels. You've done a good job. I wonder if he's ever been ridden?"

"Only one way to find out," said Thom, climbing over the gate and giving a shrill whistle. It was the first time he had whistled to Finn, and the horse momentarily froze. Memories of the old man flashed across his mind and he recalled Henry Absalom, scanning his island for the herd.

Then Thom called "Finn!" and the spell was broken. The horse trotted over to the waiting boy, who deftly attached a length of rope to the halter.

"Be careful, Thom," his grandmother warned.

"Easy, boy," he soothed before vaulting quietly onto to the horse's back.

Finn stood still, bewildered. The boy was light, but he had never had man or saddle on his back before and it was a new sensation. He took a step forward and the weight moved with him. Thom leaned across the horse's neck, stroking him and whispering. Boy and horse stayed in this position for some time before Finn, finally deciding he had nothing to fear, wandered off and put his head down to graze. Thom stayed on his back for the next twenty minutes, not asking or commanding Finn to move or halt, but simply sitting and moving with him.

✳ ✳ ✳ ✳ ✳

Thom followed this pattern for the next few evenings until Finn became completely relaxed at having the boy on his back. Gradually, he began to get Finn to move and halt when asked, enlisting his grandmother's help to lead Finn by the halter so that the horse grew to associate the voice commands with the movements. It was a long and painstaking process, but Thom was patient and never rushed his horse. Eventually, Finn was well trained to respond to voice commands.

"He's a fiery horse, I can see that, but he's so gentle with me," said Thom at supper one day. "I think it's because I never bully him or use a crop. He never needs to wear a saddle or bridle."

"But how are you going to compete on him? You don't see show jumpers being ridden bareback," said his father.

"Who said I was going to compete?"

"Well, your mother and I thought…"

"You know how much I hate competing – at anything." Thom was beginning to feel impatient with them. For once, however, they didn't argue.

Chapter 6

As the months passed a strong bond formed between the boy and the horse. Finn gave Thom a focus in his life. And as his self-confidence grew, the bullying at school stopped. He wondered if part of that was due to the fact that a group of boys in his class had encountered him out riding one day and were impressed and surprised that this frail boy could handle such a big, powerful stallion. But although school improved, his parents' nagging got worse.

One Saturday afternoon, when his parents were shopping, he confided to his grandmother.

"Mom and Dad keep going on about the future and

my career. They're obsessed with exam results and qualifications. It's driving me crazy."

"I know it's irritating, Thom, but they're only thinking about you. You can't get on in life without qualifications," replied Gran.

Thom grunted. "It depends what you mean by getting on. Granddad didn't have any qualifications, and it didn't stop him from being a farmer, did it?"

Gran said nothing.

"I'll be lucky if I pass one exam, let alone the eight that Mom and Dad are aiming for," Thom continued. "Anyway, all I want is to live with you and Finn, just the three of us. We could open an animal sanctuary and care for sick and unwanted creatures."

Gran smiled. "It sounds idyllic, Thom. But how would you earn money to live?"

Thom thought things over later on after he had fed Finn. The horse was munching hay while Thom leaned on the door and studied the gray stallion's perfect conformation and his noble head. He drank in the magnificence of his beloved companion and wondered, as he had many times, where the horse could have come from. When he had finished eating, Finn sauntered over to the boy and blew at this face, gently parting the spiked dark hair.

"Oh, Finn," breathed Thom. "What would I do if I lost you?"

By now, nights were longer and lighter and the days sunnier. Still, Thom's hours after school with Finn were curtailed by his parents, who insisted that he spend extra time studying for his dreaded exams His English exam was in two days.

"I hope you're doing plenty of studying," said his mother, reading his thoughts over supper one evening.

"He still spends far too much time with that horse," said his Dad. "One day, Thom, you'll realize what's really important in life."

"I already know," mumbled Thom under his breath.

Thom felt relieved when they left for the gym and he was alone with Gran.

"I'm sick of all this exam stuff," he complained. "It takes me away from Finn."

"You think the world of that horse, don't you? I think my dear late Finn would have thought highly of your Finn, too."

"I'm glad," replied Thom.

Gran looked wistful. "I still miss him. It's a terrible thing to be separated from one you love."

Thom hated to see Gran feeling sad, and he felt oddly unsettled.

"Let's watch TV," he suggested, hoping that would cheer her up. "I'll get us some drinks."

"I've a better idea," she replied. "It's a lovely evening, just right for a long leisurely ride. I bet you'd like to take Finn out for a while."

"But what about my studying?" said Thom. "Mom and Dad would hit the roof."

"Then we won't tell them. It won't hurt for one night. Anyway, I'm feeling a bit tired so it will give me the chance to have a little snooze. Off you go."

Thom ran to the field. It felt good to be out in the fresh air. He whistled to Finn and then leapt onto the horse's back.

"Freedom, Finn," he exclaimed, and Finn tossed his head in reply.

They trotted along the country lane, breathing in the scent of the summer flowers and listening to birdsong, and for a while Thom forgot all about school and exams. They cantered over the hills and through the woods, jumping hedges and ditches, and when the sun started to set Thom dismounted and lay on Finn's back, looking up at the darkening sky as Finn grazed. Feeling completely relaxed, he drifted into a pleasant sleep.

* * * * *

He awoke with a start some time later to the sound of Finn whinnying. The stallion stood still, silhouetted in the moonlight, calling into the empty night to an imaginary herd. It was an eerie sound. Thom jumped to his feet and glanced at his watch. "Oh no, it's 9:30. Mom and Dad will be home by now, and they'll be furious with me."

Finn seemed reluctant to leave but Thom urged him homewards, wondering how he could avoid the inevitable fight with his parents. As he rounded the lane and trotted toward the gate, he noticed a vehicle with flashing lights up ahead – and it was outside his house. It was a few moments before he realized with a chill that it was an ambulance.

"What's going on?" he shouted, sliding from Finn's back, panic rising inside. He saw a stretcher being loaded into the ambulance and the doors closing. What had happened?

Then his mother rushed over, shouting and sobbing. "It's your fault," she cried. "Where were you when she needed you? Out on that darn horse!"

Thom stood helplessly. What was she talking about? Then his father appeared, his face white and drawn.

"Bad news, Thom. She's dead. Your grandmother is dead."

Chapter 7

Thom heard the words but they didn't make any sense. Gran had been at home when he left the house, her usual self.

"No," he said, his voice devoid of emotion. "She can't be."

"I'm afraid it's true, son. Heart attack." His father's voice uncharacteristically softened. "Your Mom is distraught. It was a huge shock to arrive home and find Gran like that, lying in the chair."

How could that be? It just wasn't possible.

Thom hardly slept that night. He could hear his mother sobbing downstairs, crying continuously. His father had been unable to console her, and she refused to speak to Thom. He kept thinking that if he had been at home, instead of out riding, he could have called the hospital and Gran might still be alive. He was wracked with guilt.

His Mom stayed home the next day. She sat on the sofa, just staring off into space. He had never realized how much she had loved her mother. For the first time in his life, Thom was glad to go to school to get away from her accusing stares. She still blamed him for what had happened. He felt wretched, even when his father told him that even if he had been at home it wouldn't have made a difference, as the heart attack had been sudden and she had died almost immediately. It was no consolation. He should have been there with her. He had been closer to Gran than anyone, and he had let her down.

"The funeral will be on Friday," his father informed him at supper. His mother was in bed.

Thom had not cried yet. He wasn't sure why. Perhaps he wasn't acknowledging his grief. He still couldn't accept that Gran was gone. He wondered if he was a cold person after all and felt more alone than ever. His mother hated him, and he had never gotten along with this father. Now there was only Finn. Thank goodness for Finn.

✳ ✳ ✳ ✳ ✳

The next day he walked to school in a daze. He felt numb as he went into the exam hall, sat at the desk and waited for the exam paper. He half-remembered that it was English, but the essay questions blurred into one. It all seemed so irrelevant. He put his head on the desk and slept for the first hour, and then he was allowed to leave the room and return home. He walked back slowly, and when he passed the spot where he had found Finn all those months ago, he stopped. If he had been at home that night, instead of out riding, what would have happened? Whatever the hospital had told them, would Gran still be alive today if he had never found the horse? These were questions that could never be answered.

When he got home, he avoided Finn partly out of guilt and confusion and partly because he somehow hoped it would make his mother forgive him. But at the moment, her grief blinded her reason, and Thom soon discovered that isolating himself from Finn made him even unhappier. He wondered how life would change now that Gran was no longer there. Surely his parents could no longer spend every waking moment either working or out playing sports? Gran had kept the house and family together, doing the chores and caring for everyone. Suddenly Thom

visualized coming home from school each day to an empty house and spending long evenings alone.

✳ ✳ ✳ ✳ ✳

When the time came, the funeral was a living nightmare. Once the coffin was lowered into the ground, he could bear it no longer, and he ran most of the way home and collapsed, panting, in the stable. After he got his breath back Thom buried his face in his horse's mane and, finally, sobbed. "Oh, Finn, she's gone for good, and I can't bear it. We'll never see her again."

He cried for a long time. When there were no more tears left, he allowed himself to think about the last time he had seen her, standing in the kitchen doorway, smiling, encouraging him to go out and ride. She had always supported him, stood up for him. That's how he would remember her.

He looked at the horse, his loyal companion.

"Come on, Finn. Let's race the moon tonight."

Chapter 8

"The mail's here. Do you want to open the letter?" His father offered him a long brown envelope and Thom knew it was his exam results.

"No. You open it."

It was late summer. Thom's mother had stopped mourning and appeared to be back to her normal self, except that she was still distant with him.

"As we expected," said his father grimly, shaking his head. "You've failed every one."

Thom shrugged. "I don't care."

Suddenly his father exploded, saying "We know that you don't care! You make that very plain. For goodness' sake Thom, what are you going to do with your life?"

"You're always on my case," shouted Thom. "Gran never treated me like you do! She cared about what I wanted. You couldn't care less!"

"The trouble is your grandmother encouraged you in all these silly notions about horses. That's why we can't get any sense out of you these days."

But Thom refused to listen and abruptly left the table.

Slumped on his bed, a wave of desperation overtook him. His parents were right; eventually he would have to make a decision about his future.

He thought about Finn and remembered his mother once telling him it was foolish to pin everything on a horse. What if anything happened to Finn? Then he thought about how wonderful it would be if Finn's line continued, and he imagined a string of wonderful colts and fillies, all of them Finn's progeny. That was it! His future! He and Finn would share their future. He could start a stud farm. With such a magnificent stallion people would pay big fees for Finn to father their offspring. They would start a long line of champions.

For the first time in months, Thom felt hopeful. His parents would not support the idea, of course. They would say he didn't know the first thing about breeding horses and they would be right. So he would have to learn.

✳ ✳ ✳ ✳ ✳

With school over until fall, he spent the next day in town at the career center, to the amazement of his parents. After some time he found exactly what he wanted. There was an agricultural college two hundred miles away which offered a diploma in horse studies, specializing in breeding and stud practice and covering horse husbandry, equine science, veterinary techniques and business management. It was perfect. Thom's enthusiasm grew when he read that the college also had stabling for horses and that students were able to bring their own horse with them. Then he read the entry requirements for the course and his face fell. Looking downcast, he spoke to the Career Adviser.

"I have to go to this college, but I failed all my exams. I couldn't bear to go back to school to retake them," he admitted.

"Do you hate school that much?" she asked.

Thom nodded.

The woman smiled. "There is an alternative."

✳ ✳ ✳ ✳ ✳

At the end of the year, Thom sent off his application

to the college. After talking to the Career Adviser he had enrolled at the local community college to study intensive fast-track English, Math, and Biology. He went to classes every evening from Monday to Thursday and worked weekends in a local bookstore to pay for his tuition and books. This time around he was determined to succeed. When he was not outside with Finn, riding or just spending time with his horse, he was on the Internet, reading about stable management and horse breeding.

His mother was secretly pleased at Thom's progress but never showed it. She still nursed bitterness over her mother's death. His father spent an increasing amount of time working late and less time at the gym with his wife. Thom had noticed they were more distant with each other, which made him feel sad.

This time, when his exam results arrived through the mail, Thom was no longer indifferent. He tore open the envelope, his heart racing. He had been provisionally accepted for the Diploma course – if he passed his exams. He hardly dared read the results. "Oh no, I can't look."

His mother took the paper and read the grades. "You've done it, Thom." To his surprise she hugged him. "I'm so proud," she whispered.

✳ ✳ ✳ ✳ ✳

It was a wet and windy day when a horse trailer drew into the yard to pick up the boy and the horse. An old friend of his late grandmother's, Jack Grain, had agreed to drive him to college just for the cost of the gas.

"Your bag is on the front seat. What about the horse's tack – saddle, bridle?" asked Jack.

"He doesn't have those," replied Thom, leading the gray horse out of the stable.

The man shook his head. "He's not a wild one, is he? I don't want my trailer damaged."

"He's fine, Mr. Grain, but I don't think he's ever been in a trailer before."

Finn stepped cautiously onto the lowered ramp and sniffed the air suspiciously, his ears twitching back and forth.

"It's okay," Thom reassured, patting the horse.

Slowly and patiently, he coaxed Finn up the ramp and into the waiting trailer. "If there's any trouble I'll travel in the back with him."

Jack Grain grunted and climbed into the driver's seat.

"Time to go," said Thom's mother. She kissed him lightly on the forehead. He looked at the kitchen window and almost imagined he saw his grandmother standing there, waving.

"Have fun and work hard," his father said.

"I will." Thom got into the passenger seat and they pulled away. It was the start of a new life.

It was a long and tedious drive. Jack Grain was not much of a conversationalist and after a few abortive attempts at chatter, Thom gave up and stared out of the window, daydreaming, unaware that his plans for the gray horse were so closely linked to Henry Absalom's. They had driven over halfway when Jack Grain said, "I'm going to pull over at that café up ahead. Want a cup of coffee?"

"Sure, thanks. I'll check on Finn. He probably wants to stretch his legs so I'll take him for a walk around the car park."

They lowered the ramp and Thom backed the horse out. Finn shook his head and high-stepped as Thom led him around the half empty car park. Thom noticed Finn becoming agitated and guessed it was because of the long journey and the traffic noise. Then he became aware of a humming sound overhead, getting increasingly louder. As he looked up to see a helicopter swoop by, Finn suddenly reared, snatching the rope from his hands.

"Whoa, easy boy." But the gray horse was reliving the chase on the island, remembering the poachers' pursuit in the helicopter and the sting of the tranquilizer dart. Within seconds, Finn was careering across the car park, searching for a way out, desperate to escape this flying fiend.

Jack Grain ran after Finn, grabbing at the trailing rope but missing each time. Finn could see open fields stretching out behind the café but the perimeter fence was lined with cars and he could not find an opening. Abruptly, he turned.

"Don't worry, he won't be able to jump out," Jack reassured. "That fence is nearly six feet high, and the row of parked cars makes it an impossible spread."

Thom held his breath as, to his horror, Finn gathered his strength and galloped toward the fence.

"He'll be killed." Jack looked horrified as Finn took off, soaring in to the air, flying.

Thom wanted to close his eyes, hardly bearing to watch, certain his horse would not make it. But Finn's hind legs tucked under him as he cleared the obstacle and landed neatly on the other side.

"I don't believe it," said Jack Grain, astonished.

Thom ran and called and whistled frantically, but the horse seemed not to notice, galloping into the distance.

"I've lost him now," said Thom breathlessly as Finn disappeared from view. He felt sick.

"The police will find him. Someone will. Anyway, he'll probably be heading back home," Jack said.

His words did nothing to console Thom, for deep in his heart Thom had always wondered where the horse's real home was. If that was where Finn was headed, a place unknown to the boy, then Thom may eventually have to come to terms with the harsh reality that he may never see his wonderful horse again. He felt as if his whole world had just collapsed around him.

Chapter 9

Finn galloped until he was exhausted. When night fell, he rested briefly before setting off again until the fields got smaller and he approached a village. It wasn't yet five in the morning and the village was still asleep. He stopped to eat grass from a lush green lawn under the eerie glow of the streetlights before wandering off down the narrow main street. He felt restless and confused. He thought about Thom and missed him, but he had never forgotten Henry Absalom, nor ever would. Hearing the terrifying noise of that helicopter had triggered deeper memories. He dreamed of the island, the immense desolate space, the waves crashing against the treacherous shoreline, the howling winds. The island, his home – where his mares waited for him. That was where he belonged. He had to go back. But how to find it once more? Something primeval told him to head north, for the coast, his instincts guiding him – his ancient instincts.

Over the next few days he covered many miles, staying off the beaten path, making his journey through the valleys and mountains, away from people. He drank from streams and springs, ate what he could find. Sometimes he would stand on a hilltop, scanning the surrounding area, hoping for a familiar scent or sight. The sea, perhaps? A mare? The foals, his children? But he was alone, a solitary creature with a long way to travel.

As the season changed, the weather grew colder and his winter coat grew thick and long to protect him from the impending snow. Soon good grass was hard to find, the hard baked ground offering only stringy threads of yellowy brown. Late one afternoon, when the wind was raging and icy beads of hailstorm stung his eyes, Finn sought the shelter of a dense wood, squeezing through brambles and hedges to seek some respite from the debilitating weather. He was cold and hungry. Very hungry. He spent some time huddled under the trees, alternately resting a hind leg as he dozed intermittently, but only a heartbeat away from complete alertness should the situation demand it. However, his empty belly urged him to leave this temporary security to find more food. As he pushed on through the brambles he came to a clearing in the center of the woods and, unexpectedly, a house.

It was a rundown place, more of a log cabin, with a white picket fence bordering it which enclosed a surprisingly neat garden, with regimental rows of flowerbeds and shrubs. He hesitated. A house meant people. Would they be friendly or hostile? He had been chased out of several gardens in his travels by irate humans, sometimes waving brooms or rakes and making a lot of noise. But there was no light coming from this place so maybe it would be safe to come closer. He took a few steps forward, sniffing the air. Finding a gap in the fence he ventured into the tidy garden in search of decent grass. So engrossed was he in finding what he sought that he did not notice the curtains parting in the kitchen window.

Sylvie Mallory looked older than her twenty-one years. She had always been shy and reserved, so when her childhood sweetheart had married her when she was only eighteen and then whisked her away to this romantic hideaway cabin to spend their lives together, she couldn't have been happier. All they needed was each other. Throughout her short life, Sylvie had grown used to other children regarding her as a bit weird; "freaky," they called her. But Scott was different. He thought she was strange, just like everyone else, but he liked that. They became best friends in their early teens, sharing their dreams and hopes. Sylvie sometimes had an uncanny sixth sense about things, which some found disconcerting. Her parents had never really believed her when she had her dreams, or visions, as Scott called them. As she grew older they became less frequent. Sometimes they were joyful, at other times disturbing. They usually anticipated some future event, mostly in a small way, although she had a premonition of her father falling off a ladder and breaking his arm, and of her mother winning a trip in a contest. She also dreamed about a local plane crash before it happened. This vision she chose not to divulge to a soul, not even Scott. As her contentment with Scott grew stronger, the dreams stopped, and she was glad.

Scott was a writer, and she a gardener. It was perfect. She would tend her flowers and plants while he toiled on the computer, emailing his novel bit by bit to his agent. He was going to write a bestseller, he said, and she was certain he could do it. Their home became a cocoon which they only left to drive into town to get food and go shopping and occasionally see a movie or eat out. It was on one of these excursions that the tragedy occurred, although no dream came to warn her. They had been driving back to their cabin, along deserted unlit roads when the truck had appeared, careering toward them, much too fast. The driver seemed unable to control it, and she later learned that its brakes had failed. The two vehicles had collided head on. Scott and the truck driver were killed instantly. She had to be cut from the wreckage and spent weeks in intensive care. Her legs had been shattered. All she had left of Scott was their home in the woods, and once she had discharged herself from hospital she returned home and stayed there. She had not left the house for two years. Occasionally, she had visits from health workers, and she ordered all her shopping via the Internet, which was delivered to the place once a week. Her parents had pleaded with her to come back and live with them but she refused, preferring to manage by herself, and her own company. Besides, after a while she felt unable to leave the cabin without panicking.

She never went further than her little garden, which she still managed to care for. Although her wheelchair was her most constant companion, she was able to walk a little with crutches. Her health worker told her she was agoraphobic, which she explained meant a fear of open spaces and crowds, but there was no need to leave the house, so what did that matter to her? She derived great pleasure from watching the birds in her garden and regularly put out food for them. The horse was a real surprise visitor.

She watched him for some time, still and silent. He was thin but beautiful, with a noble head and strong legs. She wondered where he had come from. Slowly, she spun her wheelchair around and went to the pantry to fetch a bag of carrots. Then she opened the back door.

The horse looked up and froze, their eyes locking. She thought for a minute that he would run away before she could put the food down.

"Easy there," she soothed, her voice sweet and calm.

Finn regarded her with curiosity. He had never seen a wheelchair before and he wasn't sure whether to be alarmed. But there was something about the girl that was oddly mesmerizing. Her eyes met his, bright, emerald green, her hair long and soft over her shoulders, shiny

and golden. He stood his ground and she emptied the bag
of carrots on the path, then turned and closed the door.

He finished the carrots quickly while she watched
from the window, wondering what she had left to give.
Puttering around the kitchen she picked up half of a stale
bread loaf, broke it into pieces and threw it out of the
window. Finn was halfway through the bread when a
hunting owl dive-bombed the horse, startling him. Quick
as a flash he was gone, leaving Sylvie alone again.

The next morning, when Sylvie was in the garden refilling
the bird feeder, she heard a rustling sound from the edge
of the woods and made out the outline of a gray horse, half
concealed by the trees. She smiled. He had come back. He
wanted more food, so she would have to get something for
him. Hobbling into the house on her crutches, she raided the
fruit bowl and tossed a pile of apples over her garden fence.
Once more, not wanting to crowd her visitor, she returned to
the house to watch him eat. She felt warm inside. It felt good
to do something useful, but if the horse came back again she
would have nothing left to give unless she took action.

She turned on her laptop and soon had the number of
a business that supplied hay. She dialed the number and
asked for an immediate delivery.

However, the hay didn't arrive for several hours, and by then the horse had gone again. Sylvie was annoyed. What if he didn't return again?

"You took your time," she said sharply to the young black-haired deliveryman.

"And good day to you, too," he replied, still remaining cheerful despite her unnecessary rudeness. She was pretty, he thought, if unfriendly.

"I wanted you here sooner. You might be too late," she said.

He shrugged. "I got lost. This place isn't exactly easy to find, and my boss's directions were hopeless. Too late? Why? What do you mean?"

She regarded him cautiously. He had warm brown eyes and a kind smile. He seemed genuine. But she wasn't ready to trust him with her secret horse.

"It doesn't matter."

"So where do you want me to put the hay?"

"In the barn. I cleared a space. I'll show you." She wheeled her chair down the path. He had not stared at her wheelchair as most people did.

"I can manage," he said. "Just point me in the right direction."

When he returned she thanked him. She liked the

79

way he smiled and thought about offering him a cup of coffee, but she decided against it and he went away, singing to himself. Before he disappeared from view he turned to her and said with a cheeky grin, "By the way, my name's Ryan."

Finn had not ventured far away. He had gone off in search of better grass, but the beating rain that night soon brought him back to the shelter of the woods. He remembered where he had gotten food before and crept back stealthily to the log cabin in the dark. As he drew near, he caught the welcome smell of fresh hay. His ears pricked and his nose led him to the porch, where Sylvie had left one bale of hay, under cover of three sides to protect it from the rain but open at the front so he could access it easily. It was closer to the house than he would have liked, but there were no lights on, and he was very hungry, so he stretched his neck forward and ate.

Sylvie watched in silence from her window and felt happy.

The horse visited daily, and soon the hay was all gone so she ordered more. A little part of her was looking forward to seeing Ryan again. He had been cheerful and friendly. So when the man walking up the path turned out to be stocky, middle aged and balding, she felt disappointed. She wanted to ask where Ryan was, but her shyness prevented her from saying more than, "Thank you" as the hay was taken into the barn.

"Your roof is leaking, Miss," he pointed out. "I can recommend someone to fix it for you if you like."

"It's okay. I'll deal with it," she said quietly.

There had been enough visitors recently; she didn't want another stranger coming around.

She had taken to drawing pencil sketches of the stallion from her porch when he visited, trying to capture the essence of this wonderful creature.

One morning after she had spent a pleasant few hours with her sketchpad and the horse had left, she was gathering her drawings when she heard footsteps on the path. She looked up. To her surprise, it was Ryan.

"What are you doing here?" she asked, sounding more curt than she had intended.

"Polite as ever," he joked. "The boss said your barn roof needs fixing so I thought since I was passing this way, I would check it out for you."

Sylvie stared at him, her mouth gaping.

"Got my tools in the truck, so it's no trouble," he continued.

"That's very kind of you," she said uncertainly.

"I'll get a move on, then," he said, and he disappeared in the direction of the barn.

She left him to it for a while before deciding it would be good manners to offer him a drink. Using her crutches, she made her way slowly down the path. "Would you like coffee?" she shouted.

"That'd be great," he called back. "Any cookies?"

She couldn't help laughing to herself. He was a brash guy.

When he had finished working he sauntered over to the house and knocked politely on the open kitchen door.

"All done," he said. "It didn't take long at all."

"I appreciate it," she replied, gathering up her sketches to put away in the drawer. But she stumbled, and pieces of paper went flying, scattering on the tiled floor.

"Here, let me help," he offered, abandoning his coffee to pick them up. "Wow, these are really good. You did these?"

She blushed. "Yes. Just a few scribbles."

"They're great. You have talent."

Sylvie felt uncomfortable. She wasn't used to having such close contact with anyone. She switched the radio on to fill the awkward silence.

Ryan guessed she wasn't used to company. "Hey, I'll

drink up and be gone in a minute, out of your hair." How could he break through her painful shyness, he wondered?

"Sorry, I'm not much for conversation," she said.

He shrugged. "That's okay. We're all different. That any particular horse you've been drawing?"

"Not really. Just out of my head, you know, my imagination."

"Okay. Thought it might have been the horse we've been supplying the hay for."

She turned away and he picked up his cue to leave.

"See you again soon," he said. "Thanks for the coffee."

"You're welcome."

As he set off down the path, tool bag in his hand, Ryan started to whistle. Finn, who was on the other side of the woods, heard the sound and felt stirred. Thom used to whistle. So did Henry Absalom. Were they here? The stallion lifted his head, ears alert. He had to find out.

When the silver gray horse emerged from the trees, blocking Ryan's path, Sylvie felt a wave of dismay. Her secret would be out. Ryan would tell everyone and they would want to take the horse away, spoil it all for her.

Seeing the horse, Ryan stopped dead in his tracks. "Wow."

He knew at once it was the horse in Sylvie's sketches. "You are a beauty all right."

Finn stopped too. This was not what he had expected. The two regarded each other for a moment more, and then Finn turned on his heels and disappeared into the woods again.

Ryan spun around to look at Sylvie. She stared back, her expression full of sadness and defeat. Then she turned, went into her house and closed the door.

That night, Finn made his last visit to Sylvie. She was out on the porch, thinking of how he had come from nowhere, like a phantom. She was convinced she would never see him again, so when she spotted the silhouette of a magnificent horse in the pale moonlight, his silver coat shimmering, she was taken by surprise.

Finn came toward her, his nose outstretched, and she supposed he was expecting food. The hay was in the barn, and by the time she made her way there to fetch it, he would surely have left again. She rummaged in her pocket and found an old mint. Placing it on her hand, she held it out flat. The horse took it gently, his soft whiskers brushing her palm. It tickled. She felt a ripple of pleasure at this unexpected contact. While he crunched the mint,

Sylvie reached out with her other hand to stroke the horse's neck. As she did, she felt like a current of electricity shot through her body, leaving her trembling. In that instant, she saw the island, the mares, the foals, all galloping, pursued and afraid. Her psychic energy, dormant since before the accident, reawakened, and she was able to share the horse's memories. Then, within seconds, he left her. She looked into the deep pools that were Finn's eyes and knew by her sixth sense that the horse had merely stopped off here on his journey. Soon he would be gone to continue his long search. She felt privileged to have been a small part of it.

Two days later Ryan returned.

"I thought you might need more hay for your horse. You must have run out by now, but as you didn't reorder…."

"He's gone. The horse. So if you told everyone about him it was pointless, because I don't think he'll be back."

Ryan said indignantly, "Hey, I didn't tell a soul about that stallion. Why would I do that? And how do you know he's gone for good?"

"I just do. Call it instinct."

"I'm sorry. Is it because of me?"

She shook her head. "It was time for him to move on."

"What about you?"

"What do you mean?"

"Is it time for you to move on?"

She glared furiously. How dare he! "Mind your own business!"

He looked sheepish. "You're right. That was out of order."

"You don't know me."

"I'd like to."

She looked away.

"I'd better take this hay back, then," he said, turning to go.

Sylvie felt bad for being so hard on him. He meant well. "You did a good job repairing the barn roof," she said suddenly. "It kept the hay dry. You may as well take that back with you. I don't need it now."

"We can give you a refund…"

"I don't want one."

"I reckon my horse would appreciate some extra hay."

"You have a horse?"

Ryan nodded. "Bella. Been with me since she was a little foal. She's ten now."

"That's nice. Tell her I hope she enjoys the hay."

"Why don't you come and tell her yourself?"

Sylvie was taken aback. "I couldn't do that."

"Why not?

"I can't leave here."

"Why not? Not even for an hour?"

Sylvie thought hard. It would be lovely to see Bella, but away from home for a whole hour…? It was a daunting prospect.

"Maybe. Maybe I could try."

Ryan smiled. "Don't be sad about losing the gray horse. You'll always treasure your time with him, but perhaps you've gained something else. If he'd never turned up, we would never have met. Now that would have been sad."

"You think a lot of yourself, don't you?" she laughed.

"Hey, I'm worth it," he joked. "And so are you."

✳ ✳ ✳ ✳ ✳

The first snow was falling when Finn approached Harry Walters' farm, after a grueling week traveling across country. It was nearly midnight. Dim lights shone through the farmhouse windows, but otherwise the place was in darkness. Although hungry, Finn was still cautious as he walked into the yard. The smell of fresh hay assailed his nostrils, and he nosed open the ajar barn door.

Instantly he made for the neatly stacked bales of hay, pulling out great mouthfuls. The fat ginger farm cat, Roger, was curled up on a bale of straw, and he looked up at the intruder before blinking and going back to sleep.

Finn was so busy eating that he didn't notice the sound of footsteps in the yard. Suddenly the door swung open.

"What have we here?" A tall, well-built man with graying hair stood in the doorway. "Quick, Paula, come and see what I've found."

Seconds later a young woman hurried into the barn. In contrast to her father, Paula Walters was short and wiry and looked younger than her eighteen years, her round face framed by shoulder length straw-blonde hair. She studied the gray horse with the practiced eye of an expert. Although his coat was thick and muddy and his mane and tail matted, she could see at once that he was handsome. Startled, he regarded them both with suspicion – especially as they barred his exit. He backed against the barn wall.

"Look at those scars on his neck and shoulder. A fight with another stallion, maybe?" wondered Paula.

"He's probably been on the loose for some time," commented Harry. "He's not from around here. You know every horse in the area, Paula."

"Well, in the morning we can make some inquiries, see if we can find out where he came from," said Paula. "In the meantime, we'd better keep him here. We mustn't spook him. Let's leave him in peace tonight."

After putting down fresh water, father and daughter left the barn quietly, leaving the top half of the barn door open so the horse would not feel so confined. He paced around until the early hours, finally settling down for much needed rest.

The next morning, Paula offered the horse a bucket of linseed mash. He approached her tentatively at first so that he could get used to the unfamiliar smells. She put the bucket down and walked a few steps back, giving him space. Finally, his hunger overtook his caution and he thrust his nose into the bucket of feed. Paula smiled wistfully.

Only a few months ago, she would have been feeding her black Thoroughbred mare, Jordan, and thinking about the show season. Jordan had been a bold and willing jumper with a bright future, but all those hopes had been prematurely dashed. They had been practicing on a nearby cross country course in muddy conditions when Jordan had slipped on landing after tackling a huge wall, somersaulted and broken her neck. Paula had been thrown clear and emerged with only cuts and bruises. She blamed herself entirely, despite the fact it had clearly been a freak accident. She felt she should never have asked Jordan to jump when the conditions were poor. She had pushed too hard.

Hard. That was how the local community saw her, she suspected. A hard young woman. She preferred to see herself as tough. She had to be. Her mother had left when she was only four years old, and it had not been easy for her father to run the farm while bringing up a small child. Paula had quickly learned to help him, and the older she got, the more work they shared. She especially liked helping out with the horses, and when she was seven her father gave her a white Shetland pony called Joshua. He had been advertised as quiet and reliable and a perfect schoolmaster. He turned out to be a real handful, cheeky and frisky, and her father had worried about his daughter riding such a pony. But Paula was fearless, and she enjoyed the challenge that Joshua presented. He was fun and lively, and they were soon a great team, winning rosettes on a regular basis at the local shows and gymkhanas. When she outgrew Josh her father sold him and bought Bobby Dazzler, a New Forest Thoroughbred cross gelding. He was young and green, but had lots of potential. Paula transformed him into a highly schooled, talented jumper, and they had considerable success at the local – and national – shows.

Determined to forge her career as a show jumper, she left school and started to take in local horses to train, earning the reputation of being able to work with any problem horse. Her father often told her she got along better with horses than with people. The money from schooling other people's horses helped to pay for her jumping expenses.

Then, just a few months ago, her father had presented her with Jordan, a fifteen-hands high Thoroughbred mare who already had won a number of show jumping classes and showed tremendous promise. This was to be the mount of her future, the horse that would carry her to victory. Jordan was not an easy ride, temperamental with a tendency to pull, and Paula had worked hard to curb her of this habit. Only minutes before the accident, the mare had been fighting for her head, eager to take charge.

Remembering Jordan, Paula looked over at the gray stallion and wondered what he would be like to ride. Would he be able to jump? He had a nice short back, long forearm and short cannon bone, strong loins and good feet. His shoulder could perhaps do with being a little more sloping, but otherwise he looked right. She smiled.

"Well, boy, maybe you could be the champion I've been waiting for."

Chapter 10

When Finn had finished eating his mash, Paula approached
him carefully and gently removed his tattered rope halter,
replacing it with a nylon head collar before transferring
him to Jordan's old stable. He was wary of her, but her
firm, confident manner eventually won him over, and
she could tell that he must have been handled in the past.
Tethering him to an iron ring in the wall, she got to work
with her grooming kit and gave him a thorough brushing
to remove the dried mud from his coat. The regular
rhythmic movements of the brushing were comforting
to the horse. It had been a long time since he had been
groomed. He started to relax.

"You're a beauty, though it's a shame about the scar on your shoulder," she told him, picking out his feet. Finn had never been shod and she made a mental note to call the blacksmith after breakfast to check him over and rasp his feet.

"He looks valuable." She turned to see her father standing behind, watching her.

"Yes he does. Horses like that don't just turn up out of the blue," he said. "It would be foolish to make plans."

"You're right, of course."

"He belongs to someone. We need to trace his owner."

Paula said nothing.

"Later, though," he added kindly. "Let's have breakfast first. You hungry?"

She nodded.

"Good. I'll cook today. Maybe some cake." He laughed. "I hadn't forgotten. Happy birthday, love."

Later, when they had eaten and were relaxing in the big old kitchen, he said, "There may be a reward for his recovery. Mind you, I've never seen such a horse around these parts; he must have traveled some distance."

Paula nodded. "You can see that from his feet. Either

he's been on the road for a while or he's badly neglected. I don't think he's been ridden much, if at all. He's never been shod." Paula imagined training the horse and jumping to victory.

"As I said, it's premature to make any plans," her father warned, knowing his daughter too well.

"I suppose, but you have to admit, he's the perfect birthday present."

"Paula –"

She grinned. "Okay, but what if it's fate that he arrived when he did?"

"Let's just see what happens," he said cautiously. "In the meantime, how about opening your present?"

He handed her a badly wrapped package.

"Thank you," she said, tearing it open to reveal the show jacket she had coveted in the riding shop on their last visit into town. "Exactly what I wanted!"

"Good. Now, one more coffee and then we'd better get back to work."

Paula currently had three horses on the farm. There was Bobby Dazzler, now on loan to Debbie, an enthusiastic teenager who lived in the next village. Debbie was an accomplished rider but could not afford her own horse, and Paula was eager to help her out. The other two both belonged to a local businessman who wanted them schooled for his twin teenage daughters. Rab was a leggy bay gelding with a white face and kind nature, but his previous owner had let him misbehave and he had several bad habits, the worst being a tendency to buck. His companion, Doxy, was a stocky piebald mare. An ex-riding school horse, she was sluggish to ride but improving all the time. At the sound of Paula's feet in the yard three welcoming equine heads appeared over their half doors. She felt a glow inside. Being with horses was all she wanted.

When the chores were finished, father and daughter planned a long trail ride together. But first, he insisted that they contact the local police to inform them they had found the gray horse and check to see if he had been reported stolen. Paula was happy to let her father handle that.

"I left our number with them," he said, putting the phone down. "Before we go out, I'm going to contact our vet too, and arrange for him to come out and examine the horse. He knows all the horses around here, and he might recognize where it came from."

They were doing the correct thing, Paula knew, but deep down she hoped the horse would remain a mystery.

"Okay. I'll saddle up then," she replied.

Rab tried to nip her hand as she fastened the girth, but she was ready for him, anticipating his every move, and pushed his nose away firmly.

Her father was to ride Doxy.

"The vet's coming over this afternoon," he informed her as they trotted down the farm trail.

A bitter wind was blowing and the sky was cloudy, but they managed to finish their ride before the heavens opened. When the vet arrived later that day, the sky was calm again.

"You've got a nice animal there, Paula," he said admiringly, once he had checked Finn over.

"Not Paula's horse," corrected her father hastily.

"Well, I haven't seen this horse before, and I'm not aware of anyone reporting a missing animal recently," the vet replied, examining Finn's teeth after a little struggle.

By the time he had left, Finn had been wormed and inoculated.

"Seems like we can keep him a bit longer," grinned Paula, taking Finn out to exercise him in the paddock on the lead rein. The horse high stepped, his tail swishing.

"He moves like a dancer," she said. "I can't wait till he's in good shape."

Pleased to be back outside, Finn gave a little buck.

"He'll be lively," commented her father. "A real live wire."

"That's what I'll call him," said Paula thoughtfully. "Livewire."

"Don't say I didn't warn you, love," said her father again, concerned about his daughter's developing affection for the horse.

His words echoed in her head when, later that night, the phone rang and her father took the call.

"That was the police," he said, his tone serious. "Someone has reported a horse missing. And from the description he gave, the police think it could be the one who turned up here."

Paula's face fell.

"He's coming over tomorrow morning, first thing."

Paula hardly slept that night. She was frustrated, angry, disappointed. She had let herself believe that the gray stallion was a gift horse, but now he was being taken away after so short a time. It wasn't fair.

Long before her alarm clock went off she rose and stood in the stable with the gray horse, talking to him, telling him of the hopes she had harbored for the two of them, her dreams. He listened patiently, munching hay, his ears flicking back and forth. When she heard the sound of a vehicle pulling into the drive, she shuddered. She didn't want to go out to meet the unwelcome visitor. Perhaps she could just hide in the stable.

"Paula!" her father called, striding across the yard. When he had woken and found the house empty, he had guessed where his daughter would be.

She twisted her fingers in the horse's silvery mane and kissed his neck. "Goodbye," she whispered. Taking a deep breath, she pushed the bolts back on the door and led him out.

Her father stood next to the man, who was young and slim, with pale features.

"This is the horse," said her father.

The man frowned. "I really had my hopes up there," he said. "After Brandenburg got out of his field I was sure he would come back, but I'm afraid to say this is not my horse."

Paula wondered if she had heard right. Did he say this was not his horse?

"Are you sure?" asked her father.

"Absolutely. I know my own horse."

"Of course."

"That's not to say I wouldn't be very pleased to have a horse like this, but my stallion, Brandenberg, has different markings on his face and legs, and a more handsome head."

Paula felt mildly insulted that the man didn't think that the gray had a handsome head, but she was so relieved that the horse would be staying she wanted to yell with joy.

"It's a shame you've had a wasted journey," said her father, leading the man away. "Mr. Peters, is it?"

As he drove off, Paula gave the gray horse a hug. "Well, Livewire, it looks as if you'll be staying with me for a while longer. Let's hope it's forever."

Two weeks later Livewire was shod and clipped. Then followed a period of training on the lunge to prepare his muscles for weight-carrying work and teach him to respond to Paula's verbal commands. She had already gotten the horse used to wearing a bridle, although he objected at first. But her patience and gentleness won his trust. The next step was to persuade him to accept a saddle, which she suspected would be a new experience for him.

She started by resting the saddle on his back while he was in the stable, leaving the girth undone and talking quietly all the time. After a short while she was able to

buckle the girth and leave the saddle on for short periods,
gradually increasing the time, before leaving it on while
she lunged him. Eventually, once Livewire seemed unfazed
wearing a saddle, she led him out and asked her father to
hold him while she tightened the girth and mounted.

He stood quietly and she began to relax.

"This may be easier than I thought," she said. But
the minute she pressed her heels into his sides Livewire
reared up, throwing her to the ground.

She was painfully unaware that when Thom had
trained the gray stallion to respond to voice commands,
he had used special code words instead of those used by
riders such as, "walk on" or, "whoa." Thom had never
intended for his horse to be ridden by anyone else.

Over the next few days, and many falls later, Paula
slowly taught Livewire to accept her as his rider and
to respond to her aids. He grew fond of her, and a deep
bond between them gradually developed. She built up his
work program, starting with short rides and concentrating
on roadwork, walking and trotting only. He had one day
to rest and relax in which Paula would take him out,
rugged up, for a walk and an hour of grazing. As his
daily exercise increased, so too did his hard food. His

coat developed a shine and his mane, tail and heels were trimmed to remove excess hair. Paula exercised and schooled him in the mornings and then lunged him for half an hour in the afternoons. They did plenty of work going up hills to build up the muscles in his hindquarters and back, essential for jumping and speed. When she was sure he was ready she started to put him over small, natural jumps while exercising him to get him to go forward freely, being careful not to overdo it.

"Now we can start working properly," she said to Debbie one day as they cleaned tack together. "A horse wasn't built to jump, not like a cat whose muscles and tendons have evolved specifically for the task. Still, if he's got the potential and he's built right, then he can be taught."

"He looks like a terrific ride," said Debbie, pushing a strand of auburn hair from her face.

"He is," Paula replied. "But he's very headstrong. Just like Jordan."

Paula started Livewire's first serious jumping session on the lunge, first over a low log, then parallel poles two feet high with a spread of three feet, to get him to keep his head low and back arched when jumping. Soon they progressed to half a dozen jumps of around the same height, and then Paula backed him again. After loosening up on the flat for ten minutes or so she put him over a course of low cavaletti at the trot. By the end of the month Livewire was jumping a full and varied course at the canter, and Paula decided they were ready to enter their first competition.

"There's a show at Milby next month with several classes. I've entered Bobby D for the Riders under 16 class," said Debbie one morning, "There's a speed jumping class that might suit Livewire."

Paula looked at the details and agreed, her enthusiasm growing. "You're right. He would have a good chance of winning. But I mustn't make the mistake of over facing him."

A week before the show, Paula's hopes were high. She was convinced she had found a potential champion in Livewire. He tackled big jumps with ease, found wide spreads no problem and was adept at cutting corners. On a recent cross-country ride he had cleared a hedge, which she knew to be over six feet, with inches to spare.

By now Rab and Doxy had been returned to their owner, perfectly schooled, and she had already taken on another mare, a chestnut named Iris. Paula needed to bring in regular income, but she hadn't been feeling well recently; she was tired and queasy, and on top of that she had developed a cold. However, this did not keep her from her normal work.

"I'm so excited," said Debbie. "Bobby D is behaving well for me."

"I know the feeling," replied Paula laughing, "but I think it would do us both good to take it easy, so I'm taking Livewire for a leisurely trail ride across country. Do you want to come with us?"

Debbie shook her head. "Thanks for the offer, but I want to do some more jumping practice this afternoon. Have fun."

It was a misty afternoon with drizzling rain, and Paula began to wonder if she had been wise to come out after all. Her cold was getting the best of her, and her head was throbbing. She told herself not to be so feeble and that Livewire needed exercise. He walked out briskly, his hooves making a dull thud on the damp grass. Although she had intended a quiet ride, she pushed him into a trot and then canter, luxuriating in his long strides. They passed logs and hedges, gates and ditches, and she almost gave in to the temptation of jumping him, so wonderful was the feeling of soaring into the air on such a willing horse. They passed a high wall, and she felt a chill travel down her spine. It was the same wall that had been Jordan's downfall, and sadness overtook her.

It had been raining heavily recently and the ground was churned up. She tried to check Livewire, who was starting to heat up, expecting to jump. He broke into an uneven canter, and she circled him a few times to calm him down. No way would she let him jump that wall. By now the drizzle had turned to rain and a light fog had descended. She decided it was time to turn back.

Her head still ached and her eyes felt sore. She could no longer ignore the fact that she was ill, and the shivery feeling she was experiencing told her that she was coming down with the flu. She cursed. What bad luck, a week before the show. She resolved to visit the pharmacy when she returned to get something to ease the symptoms, determined not to give in to it. Each mile of the trail home seemed an eternity, but finally the farm loomed into view. Feeling suddenly dizzy, Paula slumped forward in the saddle. Livewire trotted into the yard, sensing that his rider was ill. Debbie ran out to meet them. She grabbed Livewire's reins and stopped him just before Paula slid from the saddle and passed out.

✳ ✳ ✳ ✳ ✳

"That's it, young lady, no more riding for at least a few weeks." The doctor's voice was kind but insistent.

Paula struggled to sit up in bed but fell back. "It's just the flu," she groaned.

"A bad case. What on earth possessed you to go out riding when you knew you were feeling like this?"

"Because she's stubborn," said her father.

"I take after you, then," she joked weakly. "What about the show?"

"Forget it," said the doctor, handing a prescription to the father. As they left the room together, Debbie walked in.

"How are you feeling?" she asked.

"Awful," admitted Paula, "but even more awful at the thought of not being able to ride."

"Your father says you have to stay in bed for the week."

"That's what he thinks. Look, Debs, I'm still going to ride in the show. I'll be much better in a few days. In the meantime, you'll have to exercise Iris and Livewire."

Debbie went pale. "Are you joking? Iris, okay; she's a sweetie, but Livewire? No one but you has ridden him. I couldn't possibly manage it. He's much too strong."

"I wouldn't ask if I didn't think you were capable. But

don't ride him if you're scared. He'll know immediately. At least lunge him for me? That will help."

Reluctantly, Debbie agreed.

For the first couple of days Paula felt too weak to get up and had to console herself by watching daytime TV and listening to the radio. Debbie visited her regularly in between looking after and exercising the horses.

"I'm lungeing Livewire and taking him out with Bobby D on a lead rein," she informed Paula.

"Have you ridden him yet?"

Debbie frowned and shook her head. "He needs a strong rider. We make each other nervous."

"As long as he stays fit. I'm getting up tomorrow," announced Paula.

At 7:15 the next morning, after Paula had managed to drag herself out of bed to get dressed, she heard raised voices downstairs and what sounded like a girl crying. Still feeling wobbly, she went downstairs. Debbie was sitting at the kitchen table looking worried, tears in her eyes.

"What on earth is going on?" Paula demanded.

"It's Livewire," sobbed Debbie. "He's very sick. And it's all my fault."

Chapter 11

Paula rushed out to the stable, her own health forgotten. Her father was with Livewire, walking him up and down with a blanket laid across his back.

"Colic?" she asked.

He nodded grimly. "I've already called the vet."

Livewire's rolling eyes were focused on his flanks, and his nostrils were flaring.

"Don't worry, I'll take care of him," her father said gently. "You should be in bed. I'll make sure he doesn't lie down."

But Paula was rooted to the spot.

"If you must stay, then do something useful," her father suggested. "Keep his ears and legs warm."

Paula knelt down in the straw and rubbed the horse's legs. She felt numb.

"How did this happen?"

"When Debbie came in to feed him, she saw that he had knocked over his water bucket so she left him eating and went off to fill the bucket with fresh water. Then she left the water in the stable while she tended to the other horses. Of course, Livewire was pretty thirsty by then, so he drank it and got colic."

"That idiot!" Paula was furious. "Why on earth did she let that happen? She's usually so careful. It's such a silly mistake."

"She admits her mind was on other things. She was worried about Bobby D. He went lame yesterday."

The vet arrived just as Livewire tried to roll again. By now the horse was covered in patches of sweat. Taking a syringe from his bag, the vet gave Livewire an injection and stayed until the horse had quieted down.

"He should be fine now," he assured. "Complete rest for a few days, though." He looked at Paula. "I would say the same goes for you, young lady. You look terrible."

When he had left Paula's father said, "Do as you're told for once and go back to bed. I'll take care of Livewire. Don't worry."

Paula replied in a feeble voice, "You win this time. I give in."

As she turned to go her father added, "Don't be too hard on Debbie. I've already blown my top at her. We all make mistakes – even you. She's learned her lesson."

Debbie avoided Paula for the rest of the day, and when she finally plucked up the courage to see her, Paula tried hard to stay calm.

"I'll never forgive myself," said Debbie. "Livewire could have died."

"Yes, he could have."

Debbie looked mortified.

"It's over now. Let's try and put it behind us." The words did not come easily to Paula. "Anyway, how is Bobby Dazzler? Dad says he's lame."

"He hit his hind leg when we jumped a gate. My fault again. It was too high for him."

"So it looks as if we're both out of action for the next few weeks. Still, there'll be other shows."

An awkward silence followed before Debbie said, "Actually, I've already earmarked some classes for us at the Exton Show next month."

Paula grinned. "Now you're talking."

✻ ✻ ✻ ✻ ✻

Soon, life returned to normal and training resumed once more. When the day of the Exton Show arrived, both horses and riders were fighting fit. At the crack of dawn Debbie and Paula were in the stables grooming, having mucked out, watered and fed the horses. Livewire stood patiently while his hooves were oiled and his mane braided. Then protective bandages were placed on his legs for traveling. He could not understand why so much attention was being lavished on him, but he could sense the excitement.

After her breakfast, which Debbie had hardly touched, she confessed, "I've got butterflies in my stomach."

"I always feel like that before a show," reassured Paula. "Especially this time. Anyway, you're bound to feel nervous since it is your first competition. Now, have we got everything packed?" Debbie read out their checklist.

"All right," said Paula. "Let's get the horses loaded."

Paula had spent the past few weeks getting Livewire used to being loaded into the trailer, guessing correctly that it would freak him out. She wondered if he'd had a bad experience with this. Her patient and careful training paid off and now, ready for the show, he loaded without hesitation. She and Debbie joined her father in the front and he drove away.

They arrived at the showground to find it alive with people and horses of all descriptions. "I hope it doesn't rain. Bobby D hates to be wet," said Debbie.

"I think the sun will hold out," Paula reassured her. "We've got lots of time to look around and warm up. Let's go get our numbers and confirm our start times."

When they returned they opened the flask of coffee before Paula set off to walk the course.

"It's not too bad; nine fences. Fairly straightforward, a good mix of straight and spread jumps, one combination. The tricky bit is the parallel bars," she told her father. "The takeoff is okay, but Livewire will have to spread so we must take off at the right place. The rails are four foot six inches with a five foot spread, which makes it tricky."

"I hope I can memorize my course," said Debbie anxiously. "Thank goodness the jumps are numbered."

There were fifteen competitors in Paula's class, and she was riding eleventh.

"At least I can get to watch the other riders," she said, finding a good position at the ringside.

The first rider came out with four faults, and the second

was disqualified when her horse refused three times at the wall. A ruddy-faced man on a tall bay rode in next. He knocked down one of the triple bars and hit the last jump, the gate with rail, which looked deceptively simple.

When the next rider went in, she got Livewire and started to warm up in the collecting ring. He was on his toes and popped easily over the practice jump.

"Good luck," said Debbie.

Before she knew it, Paula was riding into the ring and saluting the judges. Then the bell sounded, and she cantered three circles to let Livewire get the feel of the atmosphere. His ears were twitching, back and forth, listening to the new sounds of the crowd. They had just two minutes to complete the course.

The first three fences were easy: a four-foot post and rails, reversed oxer and triple bar. Next came the parallel bars. They needed to allow plenty of room for this. Livewire was still pulling, so she let him have his head and he flew over. They turned the corner and took the brightly painted wall, then approached the combination. Jumping clear, he put in four strides for the low brush fence and followed that with the double oxer. It had two rails on the takeoff side, so it was not difficult, but three strides away Paula realized she was wrong and tried to

pull back. However, Livewire managed to correct himself at the last minute and jumped clear. Paula breathed a sigh of relief and almost lost concentration for the last fence, the gate and rail. Livewire clipped the rail but not enough for it to fall.

"A clear round," said the commentator.

"Well done," said her father. "You're only the third to go clear."

Paula dismounted, patting Livewire. "I knew you were a champion in the making,"

She was feeling on top of the world when a sharp voice behind her suddenly declared loudly, "That girl stole my horse!"

Chapter 12

At first, she thought she was dreaming, albeit a nightmare. She turned to confront a pale-faced boy with accusing gray eyes.

"And who are you?" she demanded. This wasn't happening. He was some nut case, obviously, and not to be taken seriously.

"Thom Sayers. That's my horse," he repeated firmly.

"The horse belongs to my daughter," Paula's father interrupted, stepping in. "Do you have proof that the horse belongs to you?"

"Do you have proof that he belongs to you?" Thom countered, and there was an icy silence.

Thom stretched out his hand to the horse. "It's been a long time, Finn. I've looked everywhere," he murmured and the horse nuzzled his hair.

Paula felt her stomach churning. She felt sick. The horse knew him.

Suddenly Debbie ran over, waving a red rosette. "We came in second," she exclaimed joyfully, before realizing that something was wrong. She stared at Thom and then turned back to Paula.

"You're in the jump-off, Paula. There were three clear rounds in all. You'll be the last to ride. You'd better get ready."

Thom had taken hold of Livewire's reins. He looked as if he would never let go.

Paula opened her mouth to speak, her eyes furious.

"Do you think we could straighten this out after the jump-off?" asked Paula's father, hoping to rescue the situation. "We won't run away, I assure you."

Thom did not move.

"Please," said her father. "This means a lot to my daughter."

Thom glared. "Okay," he said reluctantly. "But I'll be here waiting when you come out. And if you try to run, I'll come after you."

He let go of the reins and Paula remounted. Her legs had turned to jelly.

"Jumps 1,2,4,5,6 and 9 remain for the jump-off," said Debbie. "Fingers crossed. Good luck."

Waiting in the collecting ring for the second time, Paula could hear Thom's words in her mind, over and over again. "That girl stole my horse!" But there was no time to reflect or ponder; it was her turn to ride again.

All her nerves disappeared once she was in the ring, but they had been replaced by emptiness. The jumps had been raised, and so far there had only been one clear round in the jump-off. She went over the first two fences in a daze, and then the parallel bars loomed up. Focus, Paula, she told herself sternly. Livewire was going too fast and she had to steady him, but they were clear. He soared over the wall with inches to spare and then cleared the combination. Their time was good, with only the gate to go. As they rounded the corner she noticed Thom standing by the exit and lost concentration, pulling Livewire back. Suddenly he slipped and, taken by surprise, she was pitched forward, almost over his neck. She lost a stirrup but quickly regained her balance. Livewire was already wrong for the gate though and took off too late, knocking off the rail.

"Four faults."

She rode out of the ring, everything an anti-climax.

"Bad luck," her father commiserated. "Still, you came in second."

"Like me," said Debbie.

They had planned to stay and watch some of the other classes, but a cloud of gloom had descended. Paula's father spoke with Thom at length, and finally, after they exchanged phone numbers and addresses, persuaded Thom to let them take Livewire home with them now. Thom would follow in a friend's car. He did not want to let Finn out of his sight.

Thom had been at the horse show with other students from his agricultural college. At first, when he had recognized his horse jumping in the ring, he thought he must surely be mistaken. He had almost given up any hope of being reunited with his beloved stallion, despite painstaking efforts to locate the horse after his escape. As he drove behind the trailer, he took out his cell phone and called the vet who had examined the horse at his home. He would prove ownership of Finn. Then he would take him home.

When the Walters' arrived back at the farm, Debbie unloaded Bobby Dazzler and discreetly stayed out of everyone's way. She sensed the impending battle. Paula put Livewire in the stable. Her father stood close by, between her and Thom, while they waited for Thom's vet to arrive.

"Maybe we could wait in the house?" suggested Paula's father.

"I'm staying here," insisted Paula.

"Me too," said Thom doggedly, whose self-confidence had improved in leaps and bounds during his time spent with like-minded students at college.

"It could be a long wait."

"We don't care," they replied, almost in unison.

The time dragged on. The tension was unbearable.

"So, tell me where you bought Finn," asked Thom aggressively, glaring at Paula.

"I didn't buy him," she admitted. "He just sort of turned up here."

"Sort of turned up?" repeated Thom, mocking her. "Oh yeah, right. That sounds likely. Not."

"It's true," she said, glaring back, adding pointedly, "and he had been badly neglected."

"I never neglected my horse," Thom replied fiercely. "I saved his life."

"So how come he ended up here, then? We live miles away from you."

"He ran away."

"That proves it – you must have mistreated him," she said.

"You're wrong. I was taking him to college when we stopped the trailer; he got frightened by a helicopter. That's why he bolted. I've been looking for him ever since."

"Not hard enough," she retorted.

"I think I hear a car," said Paula's father with relief.

"My vet," said Thom. "Now we can get this straightened out once and for all."

After the vet had carefully examined the horse, he said, "I'm certain that this is the horse that Thom rescued. He's a distinctive animal and the scars on his shoulder and hind legs confirm my conviction."

"Right. That's that." Thom reached out for the horse's head collar.

"Not so fast," said Paula. "Livewire will only be ridden by me; he won't let anyone else ride him and he's too strong."

"That's nonsense," exclaimed Thom. "He doesn't like wearing a saddle and bridle, and that's why he's hard to ride. I'm surprised he let you on him in this ridiculous jumping competition. He's a noble creature – not a performing seal."

"How dare you," began Paula, but Thom had grabbed

a handful of mane and leapt onto Livewire's back. After whispering his secret codeword, Thom and the horse shot through the open stable door and trotted outside to everyone's amazement. Thom then proceeded to jump the fence on the perimeter of the field and canter around it twice before returning triumphantly.

Paula's face fell.

"It seems to me that both Paula and Thom own the horse. The question is, who is going to keep him?" Paula's father looked from one to the other. "You two young people are going to have to decide what to do now."

Left alone, Paula and Thom did not know what to say to each other. Paula knew that Thom was probably telling the truth. She could see the bond between boy and horse; it was plain for everyone to see. It hurt her to acknowledge that. Thom, also, realized that the girl and horse shared a special connection, otherwise she would not have been able to take him over a show jumping course. He could tell that she adored the horse. But he felt jealous. This was a no-win situation.

Paula broke the silence. "So how do we resolve this?" There was an edge to her voice.

"What is there to resolve? He's my horse," Thom replied, his eyes hard.

Paula's determination strengthened. "I'll fight you. It will go through the courts. And I'll win." She was shaking with anger.

Hearing her words, Thom began to feel insecure and wondered if she was right; maybe she would get to keep his beloved stallion. He had not imagined a court battle. Impulsively, he jumped on Finn's back again.

"What are you playing at? Get off!" yelled Paula angrily.

"You'll never have him," Thom muttered under his breath.

Paula abruptly raised her hand to grasp the head collar and, startled by this, and the shouting, Finn reared and Thom slid onto the ground. Paula made another grab for the horse, but missed. Struggling to his feet, Thom pushed her out of the way as she made a further attempt. Suddenly the horse was away, galloping across the yard, over the gate and toward the hills. For a moment they looked at each other, aghast. Paula was winded from Thom pushing her and was still trying to get her breath back. Seeing his opportunity, Thom sprang to life, and before he could be stopped, he took a bewildered Iris from the next stable and was riding bareback after Finn.

"Stop!" yelled Paula. Before she had a chance to

think, Debbie was by her side, thrusting Bobby Dazzler's reins into her hand. "Go after him," urged Debbie.

Within seconds, Paula was in the saddle and chasing after Iris. Bobby D was the faster horse and soon caught up with Thom, but Livewire was lengths ahead of both of them, eating the ground with each huge stride. He galloped onwards, purposefully, both Iris and Bobby D struggling to keep up. They would tire well before the stallion, Paula realized with a sinking heart. As they raced on, their mounts neck and neck, Thom had the strangest feeling that Finn's journey had a purpose, that he knew exactly where he was heading.

The stallion did not falter once, galloping tirelessly toward the coast, continuing to increase the distance between himself and his pursuers. Just as Paula thought that Bobby D would give up, his energy flagging, the stallion stopped in his tracks. They both reined in and dismounted, wondering why the gray horse had halted. Then they realized. They were standing on a cliff top. There was nowhere else for him to go.

Below them stretched nothing but the sea. The stallion was standing dangerously close to the edge. For a split second, girl, boy and horse were frozen in time, motionless. Paula and Thom glanced anxiously at each other and then at their horse. Surely they could catch him now and take him back home. But whose home?

Then Paula spoke. "I have an idea. What would Livewire want?"

Thom looked puzzled. "What do you mean?"

"He's lived with both of us. We both love him and want what's best for him. So maybe we should let him choose."

Thom considered her words. He could see her point. He wanted the best for Finn, who had helped him when his own life was so troubled. But what if the horse chose Paula? How would he cope with that? Could he accept such an outcome? No doubt Paula was having the same concerns.

Suddenly, the tense silence was broken as the stallion gave an earth-shattering scream, standing up on his hind legs, his magnificence outlined against the evening sky.

They both saw for the first time the real wild stallion.

Afraid of what might happen, Thom gave a shrill whistle and Finn pricked his ears and turned toward the boy. Then Paula called "Livewire" and he was distracted. He changed direction and Thom whistled again. Paula called louder. The confused horse paced up and down amid the contradictory instructions. He looked at the two people, both desperately hoping to be the horse's chosen one, and was torn between them. But the force calling him was even stronger. Without warning, he turned back toward the cliff edge and broke into a gallop.

"No, Finn!" Thom shouted in horror.

Paula was transfixed, unable to scream.

They both watched in disbelief and terror as the horse jumped.

Paula's legs were numb but Thom forced himself to look over the edge of the cliff. Slowly, as if in a dream, she followed. At first, all they could see below was water, miles and miles of sea. The horse must have drowned. Nothing could have survived that jump. They exchanged helpless, sorrowful glances.

"He chose his freedom," whispered Paula. "But what a price to pay."

Then Thom looked down again.

"Wait. Look, over there," he murmured, pointing to a dark shape that had surfaced on the water.

Paula gazed into the sea.

The stallion had recovered from the impact and was swimming. His instincts told him that the island, his real home, was within reach.

He was no longer Finn or Livewire. Again he was Zephyr, leader of Wild Horse Island.